D0014393

FOR A REAL HERO,
BILLY DIMICHELE

Copyright © 2018 by Dav Pilkey
www.pilkey.com

reserved. Published by Graphix, an imprint of
, Publishers since 1920. SCHOLASTIC, GRAPHIX, and
s are trademarks and/or registered trademarks
c. DOG MAN and related designs, TREE HOUSE COMIX
igns, and CAPTAIN UNDERPANTS and related designs
ks and/or registered trademarks of Dav Pilkey.

not have any control over and does not assume any
r author or third-party websites or their content.

this publication may be reproduced, stored in a
em, or transmitted in any form or by any means,
nical, photocopying, recording, or otherwise, without
ission of the publisher. For information regarding
write to Scholastic Inc., Attention: Permissions
tment, 557 Broadway, New York, NY 10012.

work of fiction. Names, characters, places, and
ther the product of the author's imagination or are
nd any resemblance to actual persons, living or dead,
ishments, events, or locales is entirely coincidental.

s to John Steinbeck, whose novels, particularly
f Eden, still resonate with readers today.

ry of Congress Control Number 2017939754

978-1-338-74106-3 (POB)
978-1-338-23037-6 (Library)

7 6 5 4 3 2 1 21 22 23 24 25

Printed in China 62
This edition first printing, August 2021

Edited by Anamika Bhatnagar
ook design by Dav Pilkey and Phil Falco
Color by Jose Garibaldi
Creative Director: Phil Falco
Publisher: David Saylor

All rights
Scholastic In
associated log
of Scholastic I
and related de
are tradema

The publisher does
responsibility f

No part of
retrieval syst
electronic, mech
written perm
permission,
Depar

This book is a
incidents are e
used fictitiously, a
business establ

With than
East

Libra

10 9 8

CHAPTERS

FOREWORD:
DOG MAN: BEHIND THE SCENES
-5-

1. THE KITTY SITTER
-13-

2. HOLLYWOOD HERO
-29-

3. THE TALK
-47-

4. AN ACHING KIND OF GROWING
-57-

5. THE DOG-MAN
-77-

6. THE BARK KNIGHT RISES
-91-

7. A BUNCHA STUFF THAT HAPPENED NEXT
-115-

8. DESTROY ALL WEENIES
-149-

9. CANNERY GROW
-173-

10. BEAST OF EDEN
-185-

11. OF RICE AND YEN
-223-

12. TIMSHEL
-229-

EPILOGUE
-242-

HOW TO DRAW
-245-

NOTES
-253-

DOG MAN
Behind the scenes
What up, Poochies? We're George and Harold!
Me too!
As you might remember, we're in 5th Grade now.
That means we're totally mature!
And deep, too, y'all!
Anyhoo, our new teacher has been making us read all of these old-timey books lately.
East of Eden

My, what a splendid book, my Good Man!
Let me adjust my monocle so I may imbibe its essence more indubitably!
East
Those aren't monocles! They're just rings from plastic milk jugs!
What? We can't use our imaginations anymore?
So anyway, **East of Eden** is actually a pretty cool book about good and evil and stuff.
It totally inspired us!
East of Eden by John Steinbeck

So we started making a brand-new Dog Man graphic novel!
It's a tale of good...
...a tale of evil...
...and a tale of STUFF!
Dog Man and Cat Kid
But before we begin, let's recap our story thus far...

One time, a cop and a Police dog...
...got hurt in an explosion!
KA BLOOEY
In the hospital, the doctor gave them sad news.
Boo Hoo!
Your head is dying, cop.
aw, man!
And your body is dying, dog!
whine whine
But then, the nurse Lady got a great idea!

Let's sew the dog's head onto cop's body!!!
You're a Genius!!!
Hooray!
So they had a big operation.
And like a warrior born of adversity...
...a hero arose from the ashes!
HOORAY FOR DOG MAN!

Along the way, Dog Man has made some great friends...
Sarah Hatoff: World's greatest reporter
Zuzu: world's greatest Poodle
chief
Chief: World's greatest Chief
...And one terrible enemy.
Petey: World's evilest cat
I'LL GET YOU, DOG MAN--- IF it's The LaST Thing I DO!
In our Last story, Petey tried to make a clone of himself.
U
cLone 'em

But his clone was a kitten.
DNA Chute
Start
Things went from bad...
... to worse.
Free kitty
But one lucky night, all of that changed.
Free kitty

Li'L Petey found a new home...
DOG man
free kitty
...but can he escape his destiny?

Chapter 1
The Kitty Sitter

by George and Harold

Early one morning...
DOG man
CLANK CLANK
DOG man
DOG man
CLANK
CLANK CLANK
CLANK CLANK

KA-KLIK
RATCH RATCH RATCH
RATCH RATCH RATCH
Z Z Z Z
SLEEPY KITTY
RATCH
RATCH RATCH RATCH

Good morning, Dog Man!
I'm fixing my Robot, 80-HD!
Ring Ring
Ring Ring Ring
DOG MAN:

It's me, chief! You're LATE again!
chief
GET TO WORK NOW!
YOO-HOO!
HELLO, there!!!
DOG

Please allow me to introduce myself.
Dog Man
I'm Mrs. Suspicionflame, the world's greatest baby-sitter!!!
Here's my card...
...and my impressive list of references.
munch munch munch

I specialize in cat-sitting...
Dog Man
...and I can start today!

SLURP
Kiss
Kiss
Kiss
Kiss
Bye, Dog Man! Have fun at work!
Well, uh--- hello there, young man.
Hi, Papa.

I AM NOT YOUR PAPA!
Dog Man
Yes you are!
I'm a professional governess! I've got a British accent and everything!
I sing songs about how much fun it is to clean up your room and stuff!
OK, Prove it!
Sing me a song.

OK, I WILL!
Hmmm...
Just a spoonful of high-fructose corn syrup...
...gives the medicine Possible side-effects which may include...
...nausea, headaches, dry mouth, runny nose...
...and Diarrhea!

Uh---Look--
can you hand me the vise grip?
Yeah. Here ya go.
Thanks.
What'cha doing?
I'm fixing 80-HD!

Hey! Did you add solar panels?
Yeah.
Wow! You can't even see 'em!
Interesting!!!
Thanks!
Hey! Where Are All the Missiles?
I took 'em out!
WHY?
80-HD is my friend. He doesn't need missiles!

80-HD is NOT Your Friend!
Yes he is!
Here---I'll show ya!
Flip yourself over, 80-HD!
See?

He's Just OBEYING You!
I Programmed him to do that!!!
Obedience does NOT EQUAL friend-Ship!!!
He's still my friend!
No He's NOT!
First You remove his missiles...

Then you give him SOLAR PANELS!
How does he get any power at night?
He doesn't.
He sleeps at night just like me!
THAT DOES IT!
YOU AND I NEED to have a TALK!
No we don't.

YES, WE DO!
No we don't!
YES, WE DO!
No we don't!
YES, WE DO!
No we don't!
YES, WE DO!
No we don't!!!!!
Look---I'll buy you some ice cream!
Ok! Let's go!

Chapter 2

HOLLYWOOD HERO

by George and Harold

Meanwhile...
Uh... heh-heh...
COPS
COPS
Dog Man should be here any minute.
Chief
Is he ALWAYS this Late?
Yeah--- but, well, he's a maverick!
Chief
He plays by his own rules...
Chief
...but he gets the job done!
COPS
COPS

He's the thinking man's Rin tin Tin!!!
chief
He's tough...
He's serious...
chief
SPROING!
NOOOOOO!
fang

CUT IT OUT
CHIEF
GET OFF!
QUIT!
STOP!
BAD DOGGY!
WHY?

WHY DO WE HAVE TO GO THROUGH THIS EVERY DAY?
chief

ahem.
chief

Oh yeah. Dog Man, this is Sam Hamilton.

He's a big-time Hollywood Director!
Lick

He's gonna make a movie about you!
chief

THE DOG-MAN
That's right. It's the true story of a Hero!
chief
It's got depth, intelligence, and passion...
Wow! Just Like OUR Stories!
chief
Right, Dog Man?
chief
munch munch munch
THE DOG-MAN

Hey! Gimme that Poster!
chief
THE DOG
GiVE it!!!
chief
THE DOG
Ha-Ha --- He always does this!
chief
R-RIP

chief
THE DOG-MAN
Here ya go!
chief
THE DOG-MAN
chief
CRUSH
No! I can't work with him!
crumple crumple
He is an IDIOT!!!

But he's the best cop we've got!!!
chief
ABC
cookies
OK! I'll give him one more chance!
chief
This is YoLay Caprese!
chief
She's the world's greatest actress!
chief
chief
HEY!

* Italian for "hello." (Pronounced "chow.")

** Translation: Hello, handsome!

I have a job for you!
But---
You shall be my bodyguard!
But--
And I shall reward you...
But-
...with TUMMY RUBS!
INTRODUCING
FLIP-

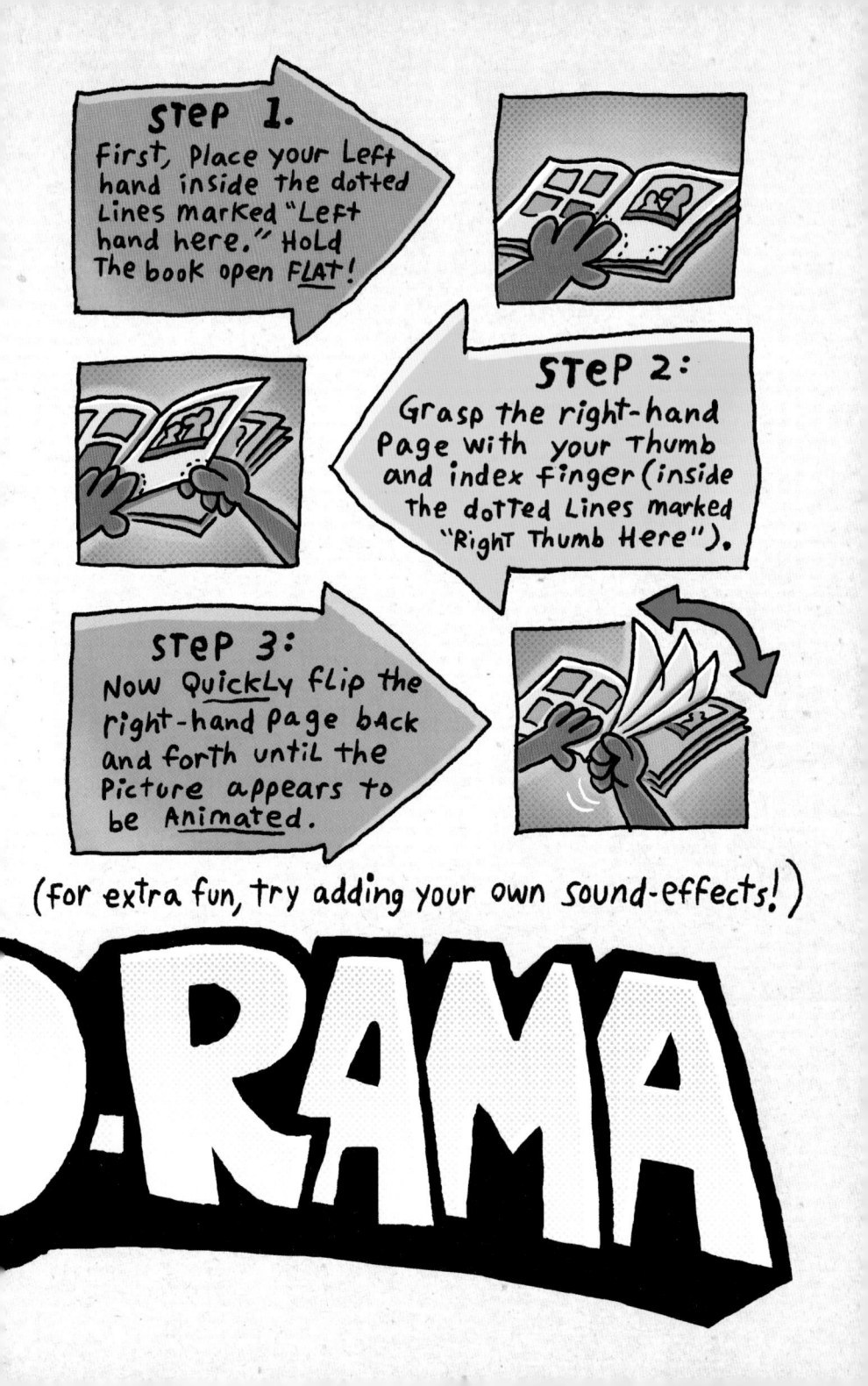
STEP 1.
First, place your left hand inside the dotted lines marked "Left hand here." Hold the book open FLAT!
STEP 2:
Grasp the right-hand page with your thumb and index finger (inside the dotted lines marked "Right Thumb Here").
STEP 3:
Now QUICKLY flip the right-hand page back and forth until the picture appears to be Animated.
(For extra fun, try adding your own sound-effects!)
RAMA

Remember,

while you are flipping,
be sure you can see
the image on page 43
AND the image on page 45.

If you flip quickly,
the two pictures will
start to look like
one **Animated** cartoon!

Don't forget to
add your own
sound-effects!

Left
hand here.

Right Thumb here.

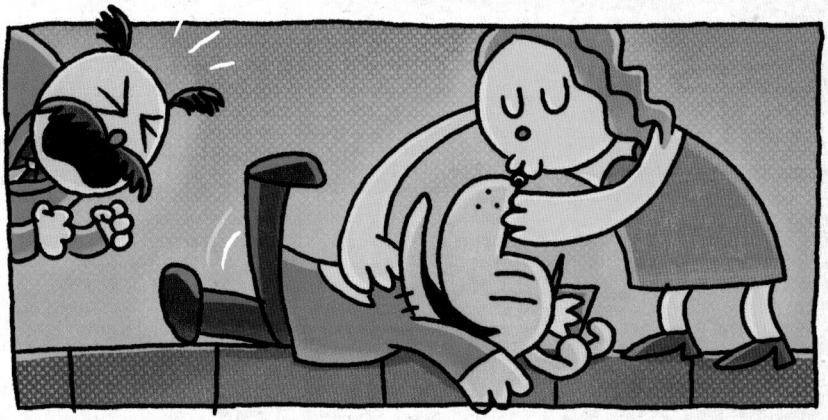

OK! Let's go make a movie!
But- But-
Oh, boy! This is gonna be Great!
chief
Dog Man's gonna be a famous body-guard!
chief
And I bet he won't make ANY mistakes this time!
chief
Ain't that right, DOG Man?
chief
chief
munch munch munch

Chapter 3

The Talk

Ice cream, Here we come!
DOG MAN
Hey! Where do you think **You're** going?
DOG MAN
He's coming with us!
Sorry, kid!
Make him stay here!
But why?
Just make him stay here--- or **NO ICE CREAM!**
Wait here for me, 80-HD!

Ten Minutes Later
Here ya go, Kid!
ICE CREAM
Thank you!
How's the ice cream?
good.
I'm sorry I had to trick you with this disguise.
You didn't trick me!
ALRight, Smarty-Pants! Go ahead and be MEAN!!!

But you don't understand how I **Suffer!**
The cops are lookin' **everywhere** for me!
They're gonna put me back in jail and throw away the key!!!
I've got nowhere to hide...
... and nobody to help me!!!
I'm all alone!!!

I'll help you, Papa!
Do you promise?
Yeah!
Great! I'm gonna move in with you guys...
... and we can continue your evil TRAining!
But I don't wanna be evil, Papa.
Would You STOP calling me PAPA? I'm NOT YOUR PAPA!

YOU're MY CLONE!
That means you and me are the SAME!
I'm evil, so you have to be evil, too!
You don't have any CHOICE in the matter!
But I wanna be Perfect Like Dog Man!
DOG MAN ISN'T Perfect! He's A GOODY-GOODY MILK-TOAST GUMDROP!!

He Never breaks ANY Laws! He Never has Any FUN!
I don't wanna break any laws, either!
But--- You just DID break a Law!
I did?
Yep! I'm an escaped convict, and you promised to help me!
That's called "HARBORING A FUGITIVE."

That's against the law!
It is?
Yep! It's a FELONY!
And Look at this Sidewalk!
You dripped ICE CREAM All over it!!!
That's Littering!
You're --- You're a MONSTER!

And now You're JAYWALKING!
Boy, you really ARE EVIL!
Maybe I should be taking lessons from YOU!
Please don't Litter
Please don't Litter
Please don't Litter

Give yourself to the DARK Side!
PLease don't Litter
It is Your DESTINY!
PLop!
My Son!

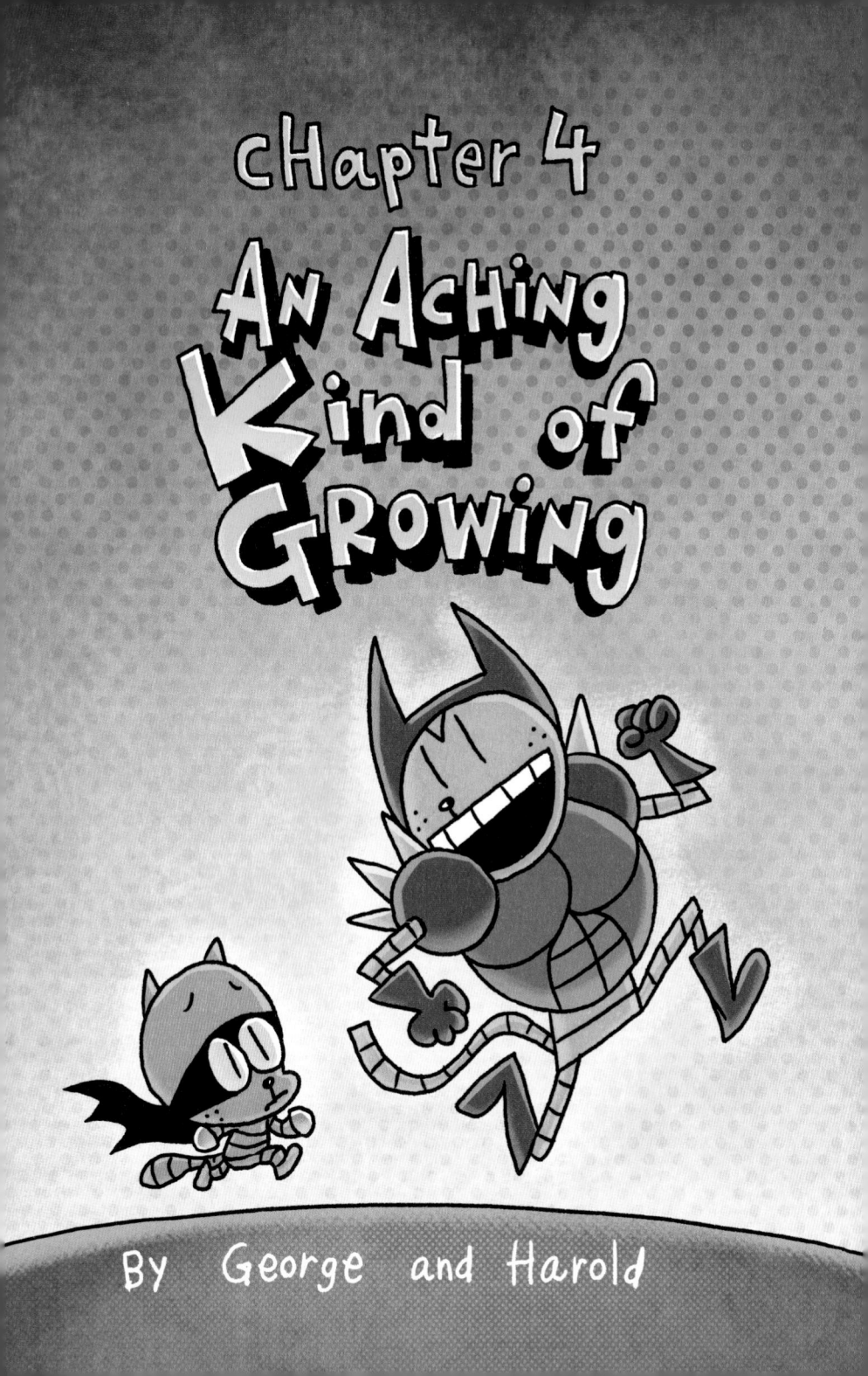
Chapter 4
An Aching Kind of Growing
By George and Harold

Hi, I'm Sarah Hatoff, the world's greatest reporter.
Today is the 1st day of shooting for the new Dog Man movie...
... and the crowds are bursting with excitement!!!
STUDIO
Hooray
Let's meet some of the fans!
Oh, Look! It's Lil Petey!

Hi, Sarah. Hi, Zuzu!
You must be the nanny! Are you excited about the Dog Man movie?
DOG MAN MOVIE?!!?
That's the DUMbest MOVIE idea EVER!!!
Sniff Sniff
Grrrrr!
Be nice, Zuzu!
Yeah! Be nice, Zuzu!!!
BARK BARK BARK

Oh, Look! Here come the stars!
Wow! It's international action hero Ding-Dong Magoo!!!
I'LL be Playing DOG Man!
DOG Man doesn't have muscles!
Next, it's YoLay Caprese. She'll be Playing Me!!!

Viva l'Italia!*
(* Hooray for Italy!)
But I'm Australian!
Here comes Samson J. Johnson as "Chief"!
ENOUGH IS ENOUGH!!!
I have HAD IT with these DOG-GONE ACTORS in this DOG-GONE LIMO!!!

And finally, it's comic Superstar Scooter McRibs!
Hiya, Dummies! I'LL be playing Petey the cat!
That guy doesn't look ANYTHinG Like me--- er, I mean, like PeTeY!
Grrrrr
GASSY BeHemoTH STUDiOS
And now, Let's enter the studio...
... and go behind the scenes!!!

Wow! Look at all this STUFF!!!
These miniature buildings are so Realistic!!!
Ooh... and what are these?
EDEN
These are the robotic Hot Dogs for the big action scene in Act 3.
EDEN

And check out our Pièce de résistance!*
EDEN MECHA-BOTS
*(French for: Supa Awesomest thingy)
It's PhiLLY The GYRO!
Nah-he's just another robot we buiLt!
EDEN
EDEN MECHA-B
I controL 'em all with this complicated Remote!
EDEN
ON OFF
GooD Evil

Gee, that seems like it could be dangerous if the remote fell into the wrong hands!
Aw, that would Never happen!
EDEN
I guard this baby with my Life!
EDEN
RRRRING
EDEN
LUNCH BREAK!
Eden

ON OFF
GOOD EVIL
HEY---LOOK OUT!
ON OFF
GOOD EVIL
Well, C'mon, darling! It's time to go!
Bye-bye!
?
ED
MEC
Are we goin' home?
No WAY!
We're gonna have some FUN!!!
COSTUMES

RATS! The door is Locked!
costumes
Hey, go through this pet flap and unlock the door!
Gee, I don't know...
Do it for FUN!
Yeah, but–
Do it for ADVENTURE!
I know, but...
Do it for Papa.

WOW! Look at All this STUFF!
FINALLY!!!
I can kick off these high heels...
ZING
ZONG

...dump this "old Lady" disguise...
FWOOSH
...And start dressin' like my True Self!
RUB RUB
A filthy...
...Rotten...

...Low-down...
FOOP!
...Good-for-nothin'...
...Deplorable...
...Contemptible...
...despicable...
...Loathsome...
...detestable...

Thesaurus
...Ignominious..
SUPERVILLAIN
And now, it's Your Turn!

Left hand here.

Right Thumb here.

Dude, we are **TOTALLY** Rockin' these bad guy costumes!
This is just for pretend, though, right?
Sure, kid! It's **ALL** just make-believe!!!

CHAPTER 5

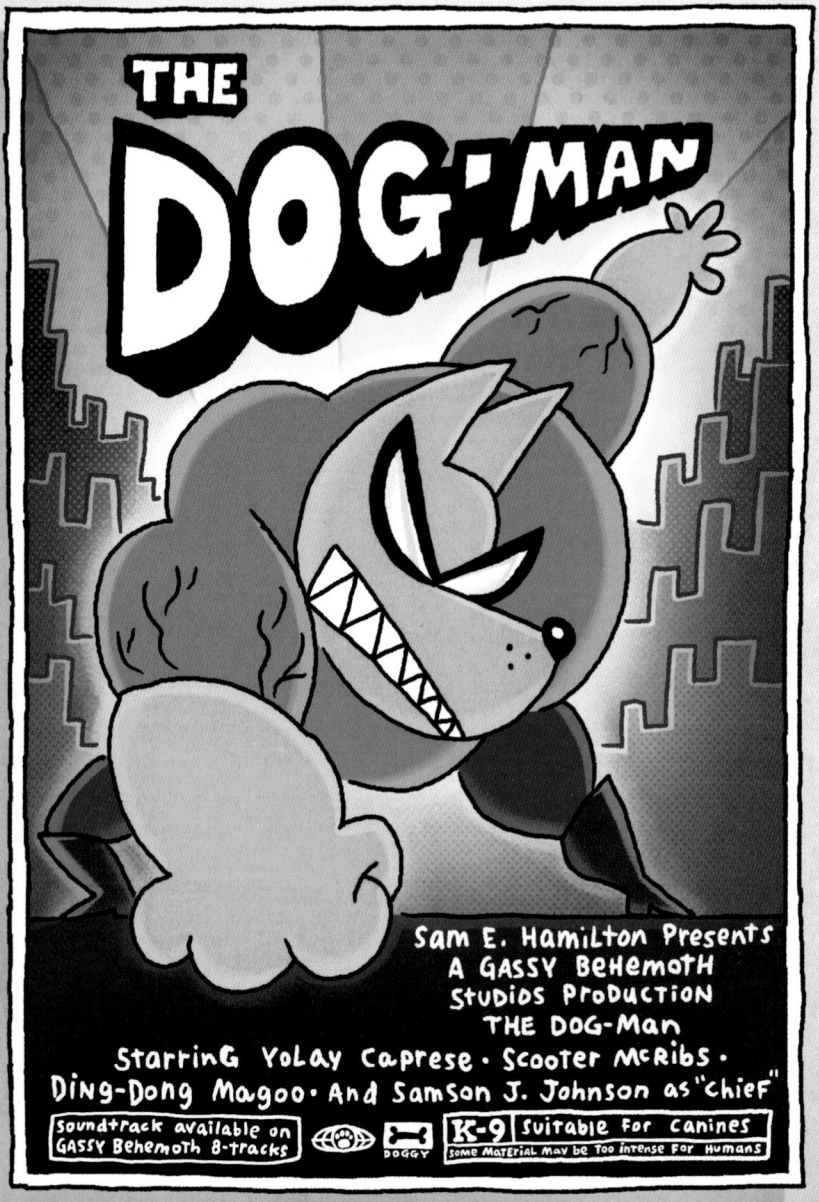
THE
DOG-MAN
Sam E. Hamilton Presents
A GASSY BEHEMOTH
STUDIOS PRODUCTION
THE DOG-Man
Starring Yolay Caprese · Scooter McRibs ·
Ding-Dong Magoo · And Samson J. Johnson as "Chief"
Soundtrack available on
GASSY Behemoth 8-tracks
DOGGY
K-9 Suitable for Canines
Some Material May be Too intense For Humans

POLICE
OLICE
ENOUGH IS ENOUGH!
I have HAD IT with these DOG-GONE CRIMES in this DOG-GONE CITY!!!
chief
crimes
Get me the DOG-MAN!!!
chief
Here I am, chief!

I'm Ready to ROLL!!!
chief
Whoops!
chief
CUT!
KLUNK
chief

BOSS
CHIEF
HEY!!!
BOSS
You're supposed to be guarding YOLAY CAPrese!
BOSS
NOT SLeeping on the Set!
You made Ding-Dong Magoo trip and FaLL down!
YeAh!

You owe him an APOLOGY!!!
YeAh!
Lick
Lick
Lick
He Licked the inside of my mouth!!!
chief

I have HAD iT with these DOG-Gone DOG-Headed COPS in this DOG-Gone DOG-MAN Movie!
CHIEF

DOG MAN, You're FiRED!
COSA SUCCEDE?*
*What's Going on???

DOG Man has been MESSiNG UP This Movie ALL DAY!

First, he wrecked the big ROMANCE SCENE!

DOG-Man, I think I'm falling in-
Sniff Sniff
chomp!
CUT!

Then he ruined the big Dramatic Scene!

Don't You die on me!!! Don't You die on me!!!
chief

chief
P.U.!!! Who cut The Cheese?

Who sneaked a one-cheek squeak?
Who popped a fluffy?
Who pinched a stank monkey?
Who blew the brown bugle?
Who let the beans out?
Who tooted their trouser trumpet?
Who's got gravy pants?
Who's cuckoo for cocoa puffs?
Who airbrushed their boxers?
Who sneezed out the wrong end?
crew
crew
CUT!

And THEN, he ruined Petey's BIG SCENE!!!
He-He-He!!! I shall destroy the---
The---
HEY!
TRIPLE FLIP-O-RAMA
Left hand here.

Right Thumb here.

CUT!

You've been a BAD DOGGY!
GO HOME, DOG MAN!!
But Sam-
Sorry, Yolay. We've had too many problems...
...And if ONE MORE BAD Thing happens...
I'll have to shut this WHOLE Movie Down!
Interesting!

Chapter 6

THE BARK KNIGHT RISES

COPS
COP
UH-Oh!
chief
He's gonna jump on me!
chief
He's gonna Lick my face!!!
chief

I Can't take it!
chief
Spare me the indignity!!!
chief
chief
HeY!!!
chief
He's over here, Chief!
He's hiding behind that Plant again!
chief

What did you do **This** time?
Were you a bad doggy **AGAIN**?
chief
Leave him ALONE!
chief
Everybody makes mistakes!!!
chief
chief

COPS
chief
I don't know what happened, Dog Man...
...but everything will be OK.
Go home and get some rest!
Tomorrow is another day!

DOG
Man
Lick
Lick
DOG
Man

RUB
RUB
RUB
Rub
Rub
Rub
FLIP FLOP

DOG MAN
FLIP FLOP FLIP FL
But Then...
SCREEECH!
FLIP
K-SHONK!
80-HD

80-HD
Primary Directive:
OBey Li'L Petey
Wait here for me, 80-HD!
KA-TUNK!
80-HD
Primary Directive:
OBey Li'L Petey
wait here for me, 80-HD!

Oh, hi Dog Man! How's it going?
RUFF!
Oh, NO!!! Is Li'l Petey missing again?

We just saw him! He was with his nanny!!!
What? What's wrong??? TELL ME!!!
OK. One word!
First syllable.
Do you have to pee???
Second syllable.
Are you drinking something?

Coffee?
tea?
Hmmm... The first syllable is "Pee."
And the second syllable is "tea."
Pee-tea?
Peetea?
PETEY?
Are you telling me that Petey disguised himself as a NANNY?
And that he was mistakenly hired to babysit Li'L Petey?
And at this very moment, he may be planning something EVIL?

Or plotting an act of corruption that may tear at the very fabric of our society?
And even while we speak, Li'L Petey may be drawn into this foulness...
... causing him to doubt his own true nature, and careen down a dark pathway toward a lifetime of nihilistic criminality?
IS THAT what you're saying?

LET'S GO SAVE THE WORLD!
GASSY BEHEMOTH STUDIOS
This is where we just saw them!
BUT...
BANNED From the SET
DO NOT LET this cop inside!!!
Guard

OK, Dog Man...
...We're gonna go find Chief...
...You must find another way to get inside!!!
GASSY BEHEMOTH STUDIOS

GASSY
BEHEMOTH
STUDIOS

STUDIOS
Guard
STUDIOS
HEY!
Guard
POP
SO!!! You thought you'd dig a tunnel into the studio, huh?
Guard
Looks like you popped up in the WRONG SPOT!
What an IDIOT!
Guard
You're coming with me!!!
Guard
zip!

GASSY BEHEMOTH STUDIOS
HEY! COME BACK HERE!
GASSY BEHEMOTH STUDIOS
When I get my hands on YOU...
GASSY BEHEMOTH STUDIOS
...You're gonna wish you were NEVER BORN!

GASSY BEHEMOTH STUDIOS
BANNED From The Lot
DO NOT LET THIS GUY INSIDE!!!
Guard
COME ON AND SHOW YOUR FACE, YA FILTHY ANIMAL!!!
YA MANGY MUTT!
Guard
YA DUMB JERK!!
Guard
YA DIRTY OLD FLEA-BAG!!!
Guard
YA GLORIFIED CROSSING GUARD!
Guard

YA Cheese-Faced WATer buFFaLo!
Guard
Ya GooFy-eyed Snickerdoodle!
Guard
WHOA!
KLUNK
STUDI
HEY!!!
BANNED From The LoT
DO NOT LET This cop inside!!!

cameras
make-up
If I see that little Dog-headed cop again...
crew
There's gonna be BIG TROUBLE!
crew
costumes

Chapter 7
A Buncha Stuff That Happened Next
PUPPY ADVISORY
EXCITING CONTENT

I've Finally figured out a plan to Shut this movie DOWN!!!
C'mon, Kid!
Don't call me "Kid." Call me "Cat Kid."
Why?
It's my Superhero name!
We're NOT Super HEROES!!! We're Super VILLAINS!

We're the BAD GUYS, Remember?
Oh, yeah!
The Pretend bad guys.
Right?
C'mon Cat kid!!!
YAY!

What'cha doin' Papa?
I'm setting a trap!
Why?
So we can capture YoLay Caprese in this Lasso!!!
Why?
So we can kidnap her!!!
Why?
If they don't have a star, they can't finish the movie!
Why?
STOP ASKING DUMB QUESTIONS!
Why?

Meanwhile...
OK, People! We're about to shoot the big action scene!
Are the mini-motor scooters in place?
Yes, sir!
crew
Is the Dogmobile gassed up?
Yep-er!
crew

Are the robotic hot dogs ready?
Ummmm...
EDEN
I Lost the controller.
YOU WhaT?
EDEN
I just set it down at Lunchtime, and now it's Gone!!!
EDEN

You've lost the controller!!!!
EDEN
How could things get any **worse**?
EDEN
VROOOOOOOM!
EDEN
Skeeeeeeeeeee
EDEN

ZOOOOOOOOM!
EDEN
ZZZ
EDEN
ZiP
EDEN
CRASH!
GASSY BEHEMOTH STUDiOS
?

How to operate the Dog-Mobile
How to operate the Dog-Mobile
mash
mash
PULL PULL PULL

Screeech!
THONK
CHUNKA
CHUNKA
choppa choppa
choppa choppa
choppa
choppa
choppa
choppa
hoppa

GASSY BEHEMOTH STUDIOS
BANNED From The lot!
DO NOT LET THIS COP inside!!!
Grunt Grunt Grunt
Guard
Well, it took forever...
Guard
...but I finally got out of that hole!
Guard
And I vow here and now...
Guard
...To get my sweet revenge against that crazy Dog-headed cop!
Guard

GASSY BEHEMOTH
ZOOOM
DO NOT LET THIS COP INSIDE!!!
KLUNK
HEY!!

Meanwhile...
The Robot controller is Lost...
...the Dog-Mobile is missing...
...and there's a hole in the side of my studio!
How Could Things Get Any Worse?
Oh, Sam...
HEY!!!
ZIP
YOLAY!
COSA * SUCCEDE?
* What's going on?

HAW-HAW!
COSA SUCCEDE? COSA SUCCEDE?
We Got her! We Got her!!!
Papa, don't hurt her!
Aw, don't worry! She'll be Fine!
She doesn't Look very happy!

Let's put her back, ok?

NO! We're the BAD GUYS!!!

We Do EviL STUFF!
But Papa-

Look, the world is NOT A very Nice PLace!!!

It's Rotten---
It's UNFAiR---
It's HORRiBLE!

And the only way to get ahead...

...is to be even MORE Rotten...
SAMUEL HAMILTON'S GASSY BEHEMOTH STUDIOS
...MORE UNFAIR...
...AND MORE HORRIBLE!

Check out our brand-new motto!!!
THOUGHTLESS MAYHEM IS BEST
NOW---Do ya wanna have some REAL FUN???
Cut her down!
Use those steel claws of yours and slice the rope!

NO, PAPA!
AW COME ON!!!
Don't be a baby!!! Cut that Rope!!!
NO!
THOU SHALT OBEY!!!
THOU SHALT FOLLOW THY DESTINY!!!
THOU SHALT!
THOU SHALT!
THOU SHALT!

G
THO
N
TIM

CRASH
AY
EST
E
B
S HEL

THOU
MAYEST
MAYEST
Thou mayest.
THOU SHALT!
Thou mayest!

THOU SHALT
Thou mayest!
THOU SHALT
Thou mayest! Thou mayest! Thou mayest!
THOU MAYEST!!!
PBBBT

SHING
SHING

SHHHHHHH
SHHH

SHOOF
PAINT
PAINT
TWANG
PAINT

HELMETS

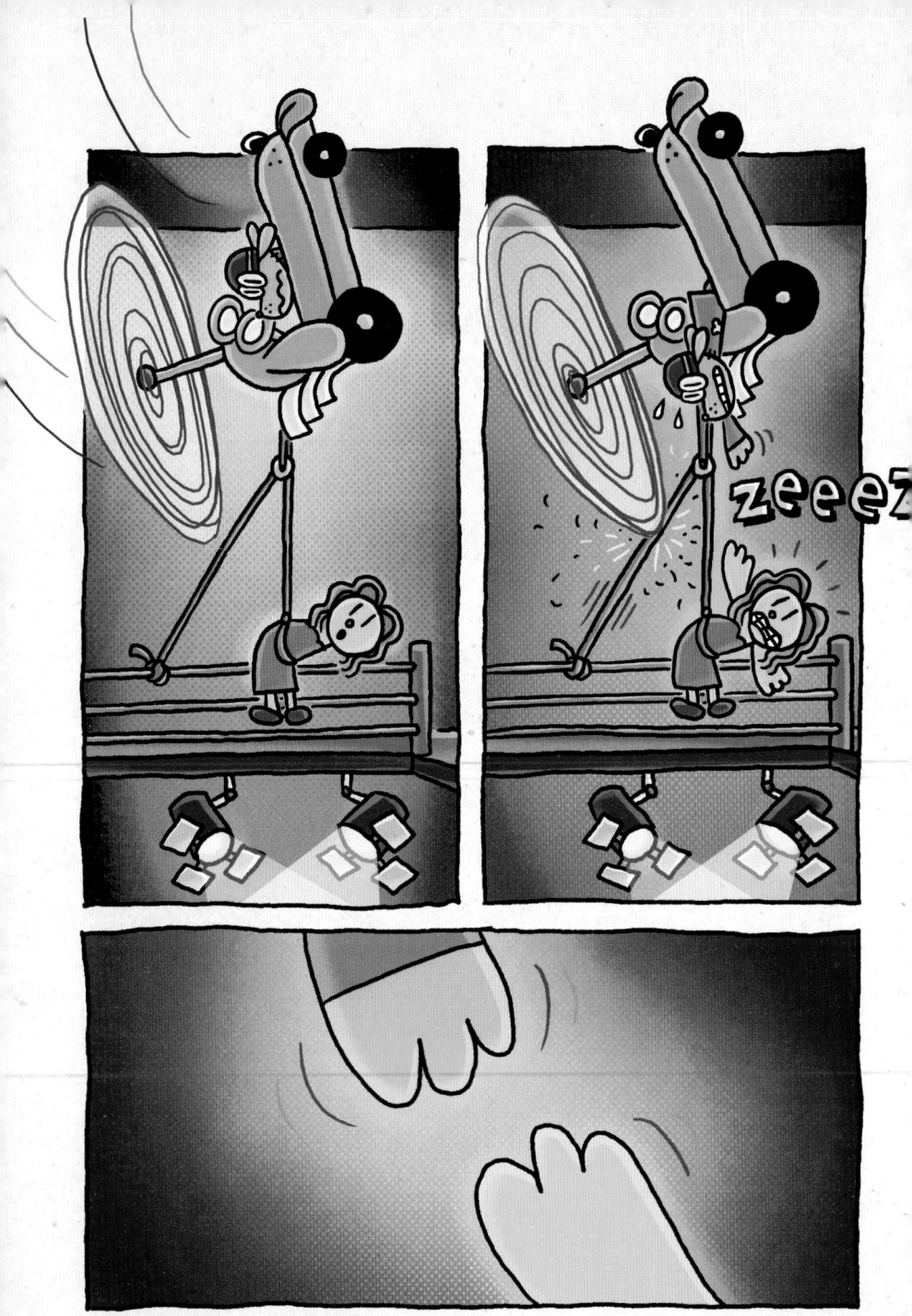
zeeez

SLICE
GASSY BEHEMOTH STUDIOS
CRASH

SKRRRR
ZZEEEEEEEE
EXIT
EXIT
ZMMMM

GASSY BEHEMOTH STUDIOS
BANNED From The Lot
Do Not Let This Cop Inside!!!
Grunt
Grunt
GASSY BEHEMOTH STUDIOS
BANNED From The Lot
Do Not Let This Cop Inside!!!
BAM
HEY!
BANNED From The Lot
Do Not Let This Cop Inside!!!
Bubbida-bubbida-b
bubbida-bubbida-bubbid

bubbida- bubbida- bubbida
FOOOOOOSH

ZAP
SWOOOOOOOSH!
CIRCUS
Wow!
Sweeet!
Cool, Right?

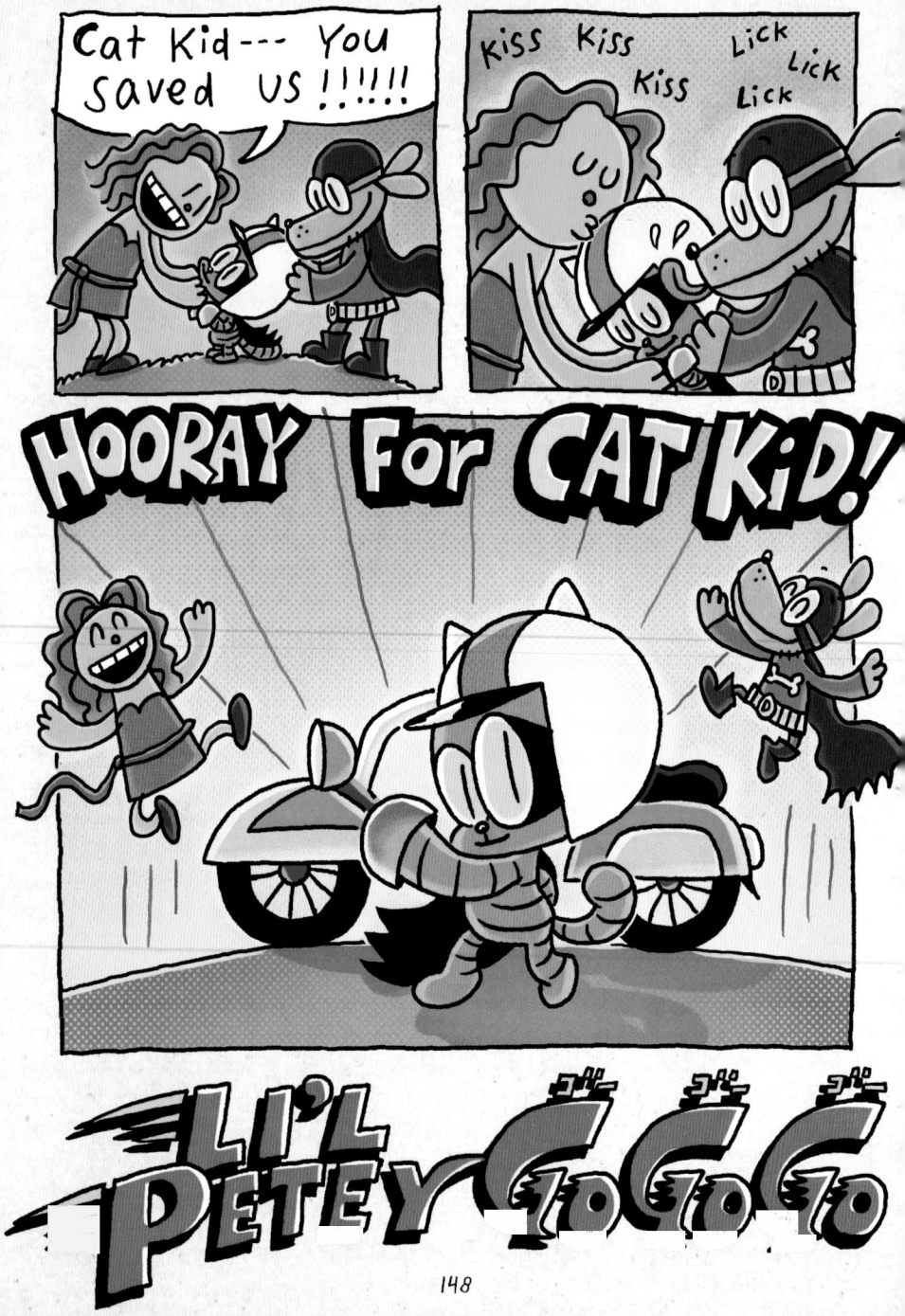
Cat Kid--- You saved us!!!!!!
Kiss Kiss Kiss
Lick Lick Lick
HOORAY For CAT KiD!
LI'L PETEY GO GO GO

CHAPTER 8
DESTROY ALL WEENIES

Meanwhile...
STUDIOS
GASSY BEHEMOTH STUDIOS
BANNED From The Lot
Do not let this cat in!!!
Grunt
Grunt
Grunt
I have HAD it with these Dog-Gone DiSASTers in this DOG-GONE STUDIO!!!
chief
I QUit!
Me Too!
Me Three!
But FeLLaS---
chief

GASSY BEHEMOTH STUDIOS
BANNED from the list
BONK
I'm Ruined!
How Could Things get Any worse?

ON OFF
GOOD EVIL
ZAP

ZAP
EDEN
EDEN MECHA-BOTS
GRRRRR
Eden
EDEN MECHA-BOTS
Eden
Eden
ATTACK!

Grunt
Grunt
Grunt
CRASH!
I'm gonna Get That dog-headed cop...
Guard
...if it's the Last thing I...
Guard
Guard
CRASH
...Doooooooooooo

KLUNK
Soon, the Mecha-Weenies began to Organize!
Listen up, bubs! We gotta DeSTROY This CiTY!
Oh, Look at the little cutie pies!!!

Left hand here.

Right Thumb here.

BASTA!!*
(* Enough!!)
I Think we're gonna have to fight these guys!
But you can't eat 'em, DOG Man!!!
They're Robots!
That's Right! And you guys are OUTNUMBERED thirty to Three!

Correction: Thirty to Six!!!
chief
Who Are You Guys?
I'm Purse LADY! Bearer of the Purse!
This is SUPA-FANG!
Grrrrrr!
And I'm Chief!
chief

Psst--- Don't say your real name!
chief
Make up a Superhero name!
Oh, yeah!
Chie
chief
Hmmm...
I'm ChieF MAn!
chief
HAW HAW HAW HAW
What?
chief

You guys are the DUMBEST SUPER-heroes I've ever Seen!
Purse LAdy?
What's So Scary about a PURSE???
HAW HAW
BAM

YOU'RE GONNA-
POW
I'M GONNA-
WHACK
TRIPLE FLIP-O-RAMA
Left hand here.

Right Thumb here.

And So...
Are you OK, boss?
DUHR--- Me Go Baby Poo-Poo Pee-Pee!
So...
...Does anybody ELSe think I'm a dumb Superhero?

YAAAAAAAA!
chief
Bye-bye, nice Lady!
RATS!

I Can't Believe it!!!
PUNX
Those IDiot Mecha-Weenies just GAVE UP!
But I'm NOT Giving up!
I've got one FINAL PLAN!

How could things get any WORSE???
EDEN MECHA-BOTS

If only I could make him bigger!
I need a super Growth formula!
Something Convenient!
Preferably in a non-aerosol spray!!!
Hey! Wait a minute...
BONK
...I know Just where to go!!!

Chapter 9
CANNERY GROW
MAGIC GROWTH FORMULA
Makes AnyThing Grow!

Quick! I Need A CAn of CAnnery Grow!
Hi. Welcome to Cannery GLow!
HI! I NEED A CAN OF CANNERY GROW!!!
How may I help you?
I NEED A CAN OF CANNERY GROW!
Well why didn't you say so in the First PLace?

Can I have your Phone number?
WHY??? WHAT FOR???
It's for our computer.
ONE-TWO-THREE-FOUR-FIVE-SIX-SEVEN-EIGHT-NINE-TEN!!!
OK, Let's see here...
Hmmmmm...

Uhhh...
Dum-dee-dum-dee-dum...
One!
click
Hmmmm...
Ummmm...
Lemme think now...

What comes After ONE???
Wait --- Don't tell me ---
WOULD YOU HURRY it UP?
YA just made me Lose count!
Now I have to start all over!!!

Uhhh...
Twenty-Two Minutes Later...
Ten!
click
NOW can I buy a can of Cannery Grow?
Well...
...Do you have a Cannery Grow frequent buyer's card?
No!
Would you like to apply for one?
No!

Are you sure? You can save 10% on your next—
NOOO
Don't WANT A CANNERY Grow Frequent BUYER'S CARD!
I DON'T CARE ABOUT YOUR SPECIAL OFFERS!
THAT WASN'T EVEN MY REAL PHONE NUMBER!

ALRIGHT, ALRIGHT!
YOU'RE NOT A VERY NICE PERSON!
I WAS JUST doin' my JOB!
ALL I Wanted to do was Help you!!!
I tried my best, but...
...Ya didn't have to be so MEAN!

ALL ya had to DO WAS ASK NICELY!!!!
I have FeeLings YA KNOW!!!
I'm sorry. You're right!
HONK RAGS
I'LL ask nicely, ok?
HONK!
May I PLeASe have a can of Cannery Grow?
Sorry, we're closed Today!
ZONG!

I'm TAKinG This!!!
Oh yeah? Well I'm Callin' 9-1-1!!!
Let's see now... uh...
CANNERY GROW
Ummm...
MAGIC GROWING POWDER
MAKES Anything Grow!

GASSY BEHEMOTH STUDIOS
Hmmm...
CANNERY GROW
MAGIC GROWTH FORMULA
MAKES Anything Grow
And so...
EDEN MECHA-BOTS
shake
shake

SQUIRT
SQUIRT
SQUIRT
EDEN
MECHA-BOTS
EDEN
MECHA-BOTS
EDEN
MECHA-BOTS

CHAPTER 10
BEAST OF EDEN

Finally!!! I made it out of this hole!!
GUARD
CRACK!
GUARD
GAS BEHE STU
SY MOTH DIOS
CRASH
GASSY BEHEMOTH STUDIOS
BANNED from the Set
DO NOT LET THIS GUY inside!!!
Uh-oh!!!

BANNED FROM THE SAT
DO NOT SAT THIS CAT INSIDE!!!
FOOMP!
HEY!
And Now, for the FINAL TOUCH!
ZAP
ON
OFF
GOOD
EVIL

Uh-Oh!
Here comes Trouble!!!
chief

SWOOSH

chief
chief
chief

ZOOM

SHiNG
SHiNG
SLice

HAW-HAW!!!!!
YA Missed!

chief
TRIPLE FLIP-O-RAMA
Left hand here.

Right Thumb here.

chief

Hang on, Lady!
I'LL get help!!!

SKEEEEE
ZMMM
HEY!!!
CAT KID!! COME BACK!

ZMMMMM
Hi, 80-HD!
DOG MAN

You gotta come with me! We need your help!
Flip Flop Flip Flop Flip Flop Fl
He's Just OBeying you!

I Programmed him to do that!!!
He's Not REALLY your friend!!!
OBedience And Friendship Are NOT the Same things!!!
Objects in mirror may NOT be as close as They appear.

SCREETCH
FLIP FLOP FLIP FLO
Open up, 80-HD!

Enter main Programming mode.
K-SHONK
80-HD
Primary Directive:
OBey Li'L PeteY
Shing Shing

Delete Delete
Delete Delete
Delete Delete
80-HD
Primary Directive:
OBey L_
80-HD
Primary Directive:
scratch scratch
Type Type Type
Type Type
These are important words, 80-HD.

They mean you don't have to obey...
... and there is no primary directive.
From now on, you can choose your own path.

80-HD
Thou mayest
Reboot
Click
Rebo
Chunka-Chunka

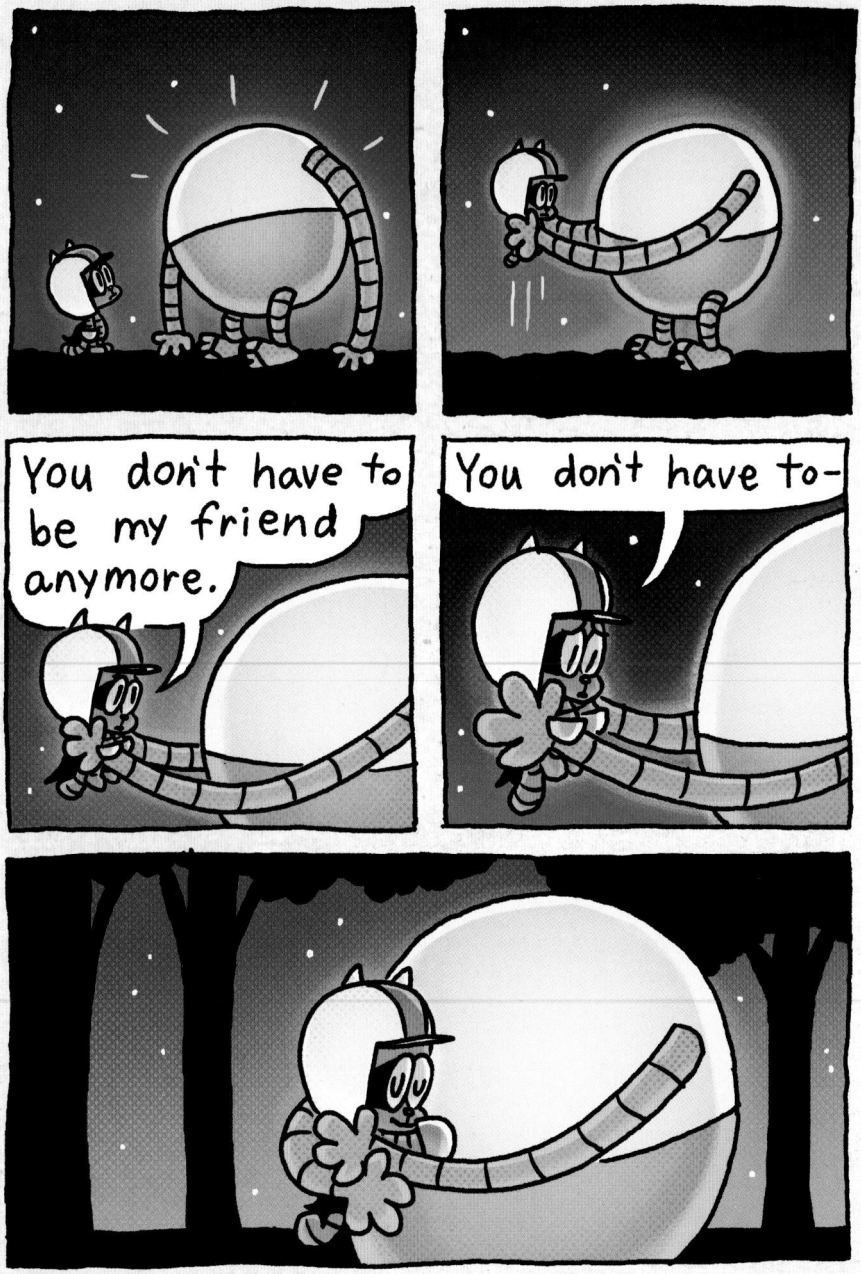
You don't have to be my friend anymore.
You don't have to-

LET'S GO SAVE THE WORLD!!!

FLIP FLOP FLIP FLOP FLIP FLOP

Soon...
WELL, WELL, WELL... Look who's BACK!!!
Zeeeee
I captured all of your friends while you were gone!
CHIEF
Not all of them!
Get ready to get your butt kicked...

...by my good friend 80-HD!!!
Hey 80-HD!!! Where'd ya go?
This I Gotta See!
80-HD!!!

NOOO!
POWER LEVEL 0.0%
WHAT HAPPENED?
HAW-HAW
I'll tell ya what happened!
The "AMAZING" CAT Kid replaced all of 80-HD's Atomic batteries with...

...SOLAR PANELS!
It's been cloudy ALL DAY LONG— So 80-HD couldn't charge up!!!
And Now it's Night-Time!
Power Level: 0.0%
What's the matter, 80-HD?
Are ya feelin' a Little Run-down?

Maybe he just needs a little Kick!!!
PAPA! NO!!!
NOOOOO!!!
WHAM!

Yep! I was RiGht!!!
ALL he needed was a Little Kick!!!
Pat Pat
WAAAAAA

Aw, Quit your Belly-AcHiN'!!!
He WAS ONLY A Robot...
Stop being such a baby!!!
He WASn't even your Friend!!!
And besides--- friends don't matter anyway!
It's All About FAMiLY!!!

Your BLOOD! Your ROOTS! Your DESTINY!
THAT's what's important!
ONE HOUR LATER...
IF you don't STOP crying, I'm gonna---
I'm gonna---
I'm gonna---

slice
SPLASH

We're Free!!!
CRASH!
CHRR
US Too!
SMASH!
WHAT HAPPened? WAS it A MeTeoR???
... A Comet???
... An ASTeroid???

80-HD!??!
How'd ya do it? How'd ya get your power back???
Art Supplies
Draw Draw Draw
fold fold fold
staple staple staple

Chapter 11
OF Rice AND Yen
A mini-Comic by 80-HD
おにぎり
100円

おにぎり
100円
おにぎり
100円
Power
Level:
78.0%
Power
Level:
100%
おにぎり
100円
おにぎり
100円

Chapter 12
TimShel
DOG
Man

HooRAY For 80-HD!!!
Phooey!
chief
Well, Petey, it's time to take you to Cat JaiL !!!
Chief
RATs!
You have the right to remain fLuffy...
Chief
click
Hey, Kid...
... Anything you purr may be used against you...
Chief
Do ya wanna have Lunch together after I escape tomorrow?
ok!

...You have the right to a mouse-shaped toy with a jingle bell inside...
Chief

IL Mio Eroe!*
* My Hero!!!

You were very brave today, bello mio!

Yeah...

...but I wasn't perfect.

I harbored a Fugitive...
...I Littered...
...I jaywalked...
...I even stole this costume.
I guess I'll never be perfect!

And now that you don't have to be perfect...
... you can be good.

Well, good night!
Ciao! Buonanotte!
Let's play again tomorrow!
FLIP FLOP FLIP
Oh, Look--- it's that guy!!!
FLIP FLOP FLIP
Hey Mister, we took some stuff from your movie studio.
So?
We wanna give it all back!
I don't care about that stuff!

I gotta scram before somebody makes me clean up this MESS!
But what about these costumes?
Keep 'em!
In fact, take anything you want, kid!
ZOOM!
Anything???

And so...
I hope all this stuff fits inside our house.
DOG MAN
FLIP FLOP FLIP FLOP FLIP FLOP FLIP
Yep. It does!
FLIP FLOP FLIP FLOP FLIP

Now if we just had a special place where we could work together!
I didn't know we had an elevator!
Elevator
I hope all our stuff fits in there.
Elevator
Yep. It does.
Elevator

Can I press the button?
HeY!!!
Grand Ballroom
I didn't know our house had a grand ballroom!
Grand Ballroom
CLICK
DING

GRAND BALLROOM
Wow! It's a room full of balls!
Flip Flop Flip
This is Grand!
PAT PAT
And so, the three friends worked and played together...
Flop Flip Flop Flip

...until it was time for bed.
DOG
Man
DOG
Man

The
End

BUT WAIT...
...IF you thought our adventure was over...
YOU AIN'T READ NOTHIN' YET!
At this very moment, George and Harold are reading Another old-timey book...
Lord of the Flies
William Golding
Lord of the Flies
William Golding

... and getting a buncha New-Timey ideas!
So get ready for an epic tale...
...of depth, maturity, and intelligence.
sniff
sniff
Because a Brand-New Dog Man adventure is comin' your way!!!
FLIP FLOP FLIP FLOP FLIP

DOG MAN
LORD OF the FLEAS
If You Like Thrills...
...And you Like LAFFS...
...Then DOG MAN is GO!
DOG Man is Go?
That don't make no sense!!!
Guard
whoops!
But We Like it!!!

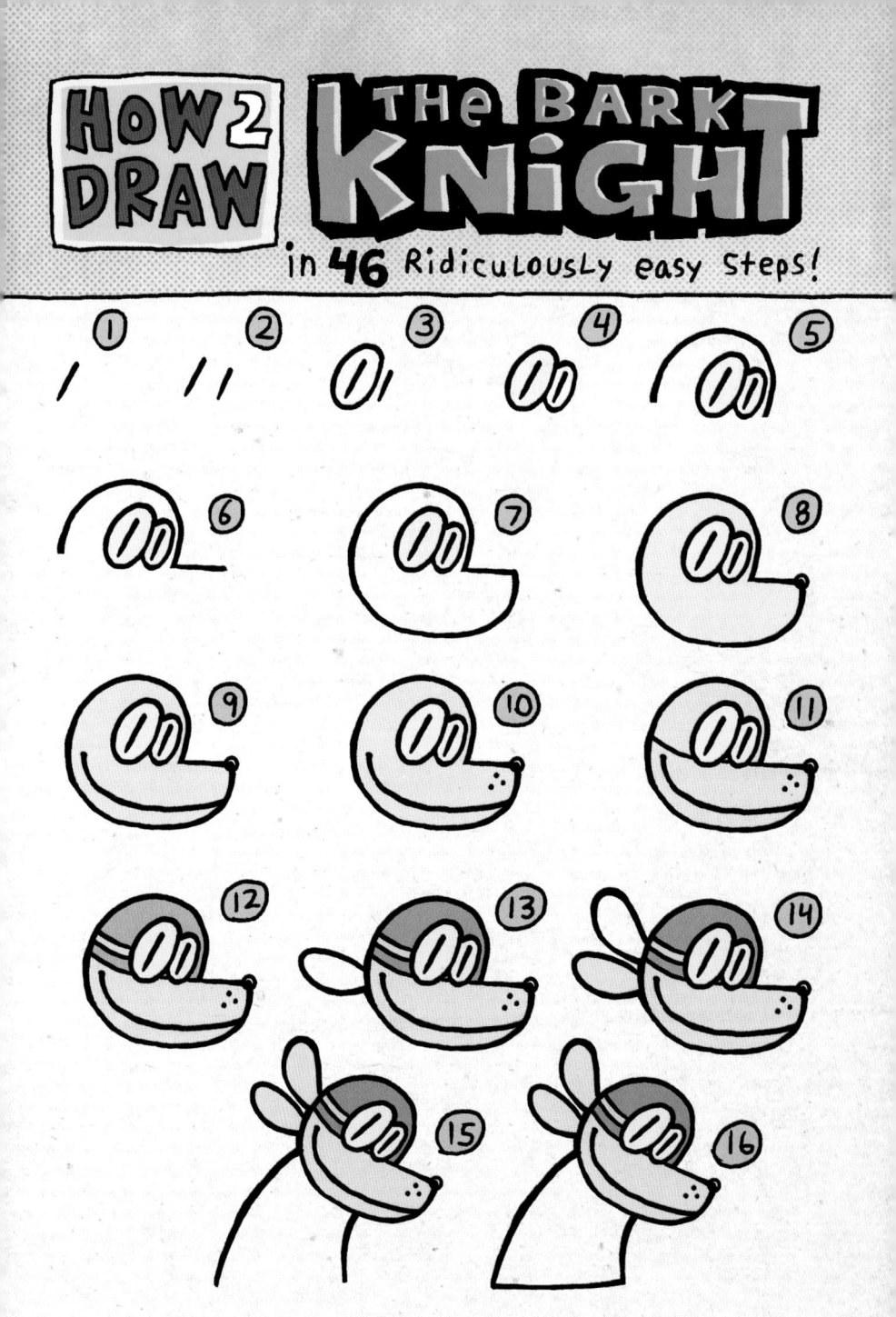
HOW 2 DRAW
THE BARK KNIGHT
in 46 Ridiculously easy Steps!
1
2
3
4
5
6
7
8
9
10
11
12
13
14
15
16

17
18
19
20
21
22
23
24
25
26
27
28
29
30
31
32
33
34

35
36
37
38
39
40
41
42
43
44
45
46

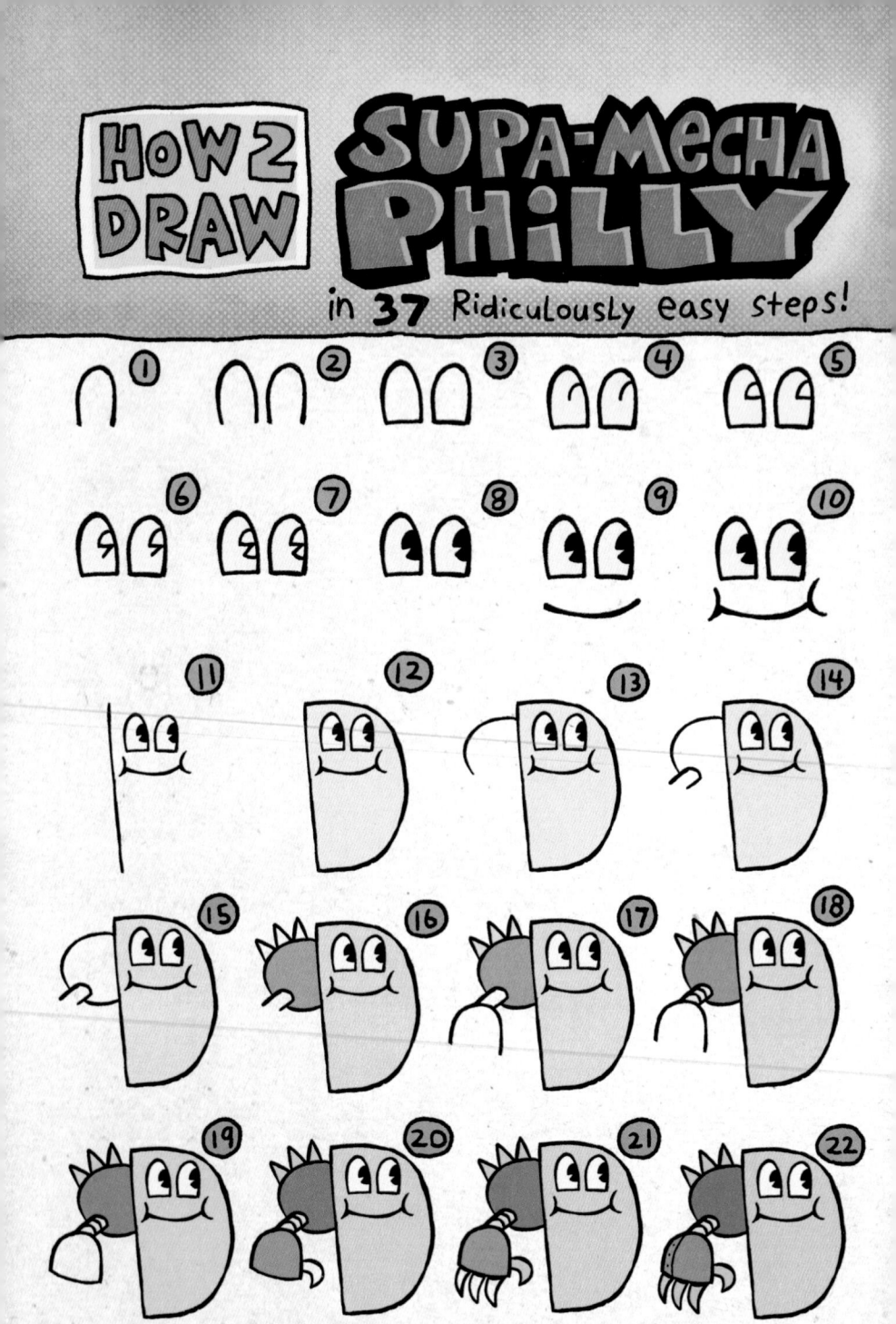
HOW 2 DRAW
SUPA-MECHA PHILLY
in 37 Ridiculously easy steps!
1
2
3
4
5
6
7
8
9
10
11
12
13
14
15
16
17
18
19
20
21
22

23
24
25
26
27
28
29
30
31
32
33
34
35
36
37

HOW 2 DRAW
CAT KID
in 39 Ridiculously easy steps!
1
2
3
4
5
6
7
8
9
10
11
12
13
14
15
16
17
18
19
20
21

22
23
24
25
26
27
28
29
30
31
32
33
34
35
36

37
38
39

LEARN 2 DRAW MORE STUFF!
at PLANETPILKEY.COM
CHIEF

NOTES

by George and Harold

★ The titles of chapters 9, 10, and 11 are parodies of the titles of Other books by John Steinbeck.

★ The words on pages 57 and 233 are direct Quotes from East of Eden by Steinbeck.

★ The Japanese words in chapter 11 mean: Onigiri (rice balls), 100 yen (about a dollar).

★ "Timshel" is the Hebrew word for "Thou mayest."

GET READING W

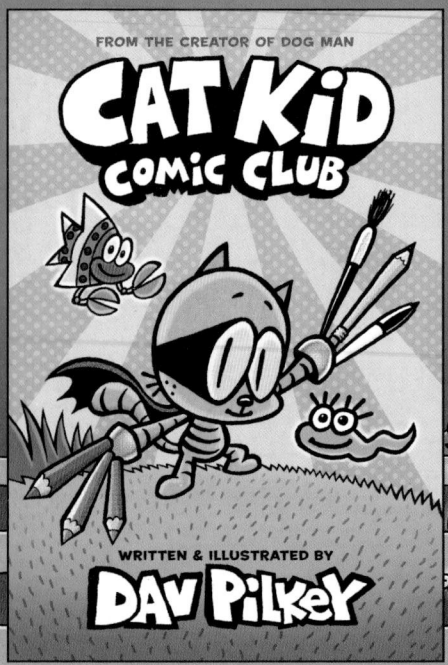

★ "Irreverent, laugh-out-loud funny, and . . . downright moving."
— Publishers Weekly, starred review